Santa's Sled Race

Of all Santa's elves, Pippy was the smallest. Of all Santa's reindeer, Randi was the smallest.

One day, Pippy and Randi were playing in the snow.

"What are those elves doing over there?" asked Randi.

"They are practicing for Santa's Sled Race," said Pippy. "The winner gets to ride with Santa when he delivers toys on Christmas Eve."

"Are you going to race your sled?" asked Randi.

"I don't have a sled," said Pippy, looking down at the snow.

"Wait," Randi said. "I saw a little sled in the reindeer barn one time. Let's go get it out."

Randi led Pippy to the part of the reindeer barn where she saw the little sled.

All that day Pippy and Randi
fixed up the little sled. Pippy
sharpened the blades. Randi
brushed on a new coat of paint.
They cleaned and fixed the sled
until it looked like new.

Pippy signed up to be in Santa's Sled Race. The other elves laughed at him.

"You're going to be in the race?" said an elf named Elgin. "You're too small."

"He's right," said another elf, named Misty. "You don't stand a chance against us bigger elves."

Pippy saw Elgin cleaning his sled. "How am I ever going to beat a big sled like that?" Pippy asked himself.

"I have rockets on my sled," said Misty. "I'm going to beat everyone else in the race — especially you, Pippy."

Pippy looked down at the snow-covered ground and walked away.

"Why are you sad?" asked Randi.

"I don't stand a chance in the race," said Pippy with a sigh.

"Don't worry," said Randi. "I'll cheer for you."

Pippy had to stay in the reindeer barn because a great snow storm blew in that night.

The next morning everyone gathered for Santa's Sled Race. Even with all the deep snow from the storm, Santa decided the race should still be held.

"On your mark! Get set! Go!"

But before most of the sleds went two feet, they sank into the deep snow.

Elgin cried out, "No! It's not fair!"

Misty's rocket sled sank faster than anyone else's because her rockets melted the snow.

But since Pippy and his sled were smaller than any of the others, he did not sink.

"Go! Pippy, go!" shouted Randi.

Pippy slid all the way down the hill and across the finish line. The crowd cheered for him. "Pippy! Pippy!" they chanted.

"Congratulations," said Santa Claus, as he placed a medal around Pippy's neck. "You get to ride with me tonight as I deliver toys to boys and girls all over the world."

"Thank you, Santa," said Pippy.

Since Pippy was the smallest elf, he would not take up much room in Santa's sleigh. Pippy asked his friend Randi to ride with him.

"Sure," said Randi. "I'm still too small to lead the sleigh with other reindeer. It will be fun!"

That night Pippy and Randi helped Santa deliver toys. They never forgot it.